TALES OF TENSION

A COLLECTION OF SHORT STORIES

Written by David Hamilton

TALES OF TENSION
David Hamilton
dshamilton05@gmail.com
©2024

# RIDE OF LIFE

(A female biker is pursued by a vengeful rival.)

Talia always loved the wide open road. She visited rest stops along a very long stretch of Arizona's dusty desert highway. The young biker had met many friends at the rest stops who were truckers, enjoying the company of most of them.

The free-spirited woman drove through the desert on her spanking new Harley Davidson 74 motorcycle. She was twenty-seven with midnight hair and garbed in all black leathers. Each rest stop she had noticed something odd about the other customers. They had all glared at her in seeming disdain. It had made Talia uncomfortable.

Her mind drifted back to a month earlier when she had raced a former friend for money and pink slips that would have granted ownership of each other's bikes. Talia had won, but had destroyed the Harley of a good friend, Carl Hanson, when she had forced him off the road.

Carl had not forgotten.

Might that have been the cause of those menacing stares from everyone? She knew he had many friends in the biker community.

***

From the shadows of a small café there, an obscured figure had glowered at her departure. Talia now zipped across the desert toward her next rest stop, some miles away. A thunderous roar of an engine -- indicating another motorcycle close behind her -- seized her attention. *Carl?*

Whoever it was, Talia wanted no part of that mysterious rider. Her hand pressed down on the accelerator on the handlebars. She pulled away, but the rider matched her speed. The midnight- haired beauty accelerated harder, more than she'd ever dared go.

Was this some sort of perverse game of revenge Carl was playing, if indeed it was him? Talia pushed her Harley all the more. She wondered if such actions would damage her bike the way she had brought on the destruction of Carl's. She glanced over her shoulder; the figure was fading into the distance. Talia sighed in relief as another rest stop loomed ahead on the horizon.

***

The black-haired beauty coasted into the rest stop, glancing back and looking out for her pursuer. No sign of whoever it was. Maybe it wasn't him after all. She removed the keys and hustled into the café, glancing nervously behind her just the same.

The café was sparse and dimly lit. Talia spotted her friend, Adriana, sitting on one of the stools by the bar. Adriana was a slender trucker who oozed toughness, just like her male counterparts.

"Talia, what's wrong? You look like you're running away from something," Adriana said.

"I'm being chased by someone on a Harley who keeps following me."

"Maybe it's Carl. After all, you did total his last bike. You know how he loved that Harley."

"Well, what am I supposed to do?"

Talia glanced over her shoulder, noticing something familiar about the figure getting off the Harley in the lot: bright blue eyes, lightly concealed under brown grayish hair. It *was* Carl.

She turned back to Adriana. "It's him."

"Leave by the back entrance. I'll distract Carl."

Talia ran toward the back just as the burly biker entered the café.

"Carl, it's been a while. Why don't you have a seat and listen to some music with me?" Adriana cooed seductively.

The biker hauled his well-built frame over to the stools. He did not notice Talia disappearing into the back of the building.

Carl's eyes peered right through Adriana. He was not happy. Those cold blue eyes could melt anyone into fright. At that moment, Adriana was happy *she* wasn't the one who had destroyed his bike. His grudge against Talia was real.

"She's been gone a goddamn long time. Where is she?"

"Talia's just using the restroom," Adriana uttered unconvincingly.

Carl rose from the stool and looked outside. *Talia's Harley was missing.* He turned back to the tough trucker woman.

"Nice try, babe." Carl turned and stomped out.

\*\*\*

Talia pressed on with her Harley, pushing it well past its limits. She couldn't keep this up for long. The black-leathered beauty rushed to her next stop hoping to increase the distance between them. Her thoughts again went back to the day she had raced Carl and destroyed his Harley.

She knew he would never give up. How far would his thirst for revenge go, and how long could Adriana keep Carl distracted back there? Talia stared out at her surroundings. The Arizona desert rushed by and she soon began to relax. Lizards and other wildlife all skittered past. Maybe she wouldn't have to face Carl after all.

Soon, though, she heard the distinct sound of Carl's new Harley. He was coming. This was it.

Finally, Talia would have to face the burly biker and deal with him. Hopefully it might be resolved peacefully; but the leather-garbed woman didn't really think so.

She had no money to offer for his damaged bike.

Knowing she couldn't avoid him forever, she rotated her Harley back toward Carl. The disgruntled biker was still bearing down on her at full speed. This was it. She could die racing head-on with Carl … if neither of them bailed at the last second.

The motorcycles rumbled toward each other like two battling bull elks. Talia and Carl both jumped from their bikes at the last instant, hitting the ground hard. The bikes collided, pieces of both motorcycles flying everywhere!

Talia lay on the road, bleeding from her shoulder. Carl approached her as she lay on the ground. He was bleeding from his neck himself.

She glanced up at him. They eyed one another for a long moment.

"Hope you don't want another rematch. Fair trade? A bike for a bike?" Talia gasped.

He looked back at his now destroyed bike, frowning. Carl shook his head disbelievingly. Was this crazy bitch serious?

"You okay to get up," he said finally.

"I think so." Offering him her hand, Carl helped her to her feet. He observed her attitude. She was incredibly calm. Carl tried to hide a smile, but it didn't work.

"You play a hell of a game of chicken, girl."

"So do you, friend."

THE END

FIRE ALARM

(A middle aged man comfy life is disturbed and is changed by it.)

(First published in Conceit Magazine, October 2021)

Rodney Bellingham was happiest when he sat in his comfy old easy chair, the kind that reclined and provided a footrest … the one that was in his living room. It was where the sixty-year-old man could cuddle with his small dogs. He was retired and was just by himself. The warmth they gave him was calming and relaxing. Every Friday, Rodney sat and reclined in that chair, waiting patiently, waiting as his pepperoni pizza baked in the oven. The meaty smells always tantalized his senses.

He gazed down at both miniature poodles as they shook their brown-and-white tails and bodies happily. He had always wondered if they felt the same about him. His dogs were young by human standards, but he was an old fart. Did they enjoy his company as much as he did theirs? Rodney's salt-and-pepper grey mustache twitched from the aroma that came from the kitchen. The smell of American cheese often drew the dogs away, though.

He sat in his chair, comforted by its soft material while running his hand across it. The older gentleman struggled to stay awake… despite the calls of distant sirens. Rodney never heard them. His eyelids drooped as though hand-weights were pulling them down.

He woke suddenly to the smell of his favorite pizza … *burning*? The aroma of pepperoni and cheese wafted in his direction. Something seemed off; it didn't smell like it should have. He wondered if he should get up from his comfortable chair to inspect it. He often was so absorbed in his comfort that he worried he might even become glued to the seat. But now his cherished comfort zone had been disrupted.

"Is my pizza burning?"

One of his dogs, Wally, came prancing into the living room. Rodney stared at him - - the poodle usually the happiest dog in the world - - seeing something had clearly disturbed him. "Hey there

Wally, my pizza burning?" Rodney asked as if actually expecting an answer.

Wally trotted away nervously, prompting Rodney to rise from his seat and follow. "Chair, I better get up and check my pizza," Rodney groaned. He paused as if waiting for a response. Nothing.

Rodney pushed down on the arms of the chair. Finally, he was able to heft his bulk out of the chair's cushioned depths. He gazed back at it, as if to say "Sorry to leave you buddy." No response.

Attending to his pizza was paramount.

Rodney hustled as quickly as his bulky old frame could carry him into the kitchen. He closed his eyes tightly, not wanting to behold the burned remnants of his favorite meal. The ashy smell of burny crust reached his nose. The old man's face cringed at the acrid aroma. Reluctantly he opened his eyes. He approached the oven cautiously and creaked it open.

A wisp of smoke billowed forth. His worst fears had been confirmed.

The pizza was smothered in ashy pieces of burning crust that encircled the black spotted cheese. Rodney frowned at the sight of his destroyed meal.

Both dogs bounded into the kitchen suddenly, like heralds bearing the latest news.

"Now what?" he groaned.

Remy barked loudly at him, Wally did the same. The distraught elder glanced about and scratched his head, confused.

Both Remy and Wally dashed out of the kitchen. Rodney followed both dogs back into the living room.

As he entered, something clearly had changed. A new aroma had slipped into the room, *and it wasn't pizza.*

Both poodles leapt up onto the hassock and stared out the window. They squirmed uncomfortably.

Rodney hustled over to the window. He gazed outside and saw what the pooches had detected.

A fire was consuming the house across the street. The sixty-year-old wondered how long it had been burning and why he hadn't noticed before. Then again, he had been sound asleep in his comfy chair, like the good ol' fellow he was. Truly ironic, first a burning pizza; now a burning house. What to do? Call the fire department? But why weren't they here already?

He rushed out his front door, hoping to help in some way. Were there people inside? He couldn't tell, but someone had to act fast.

The house was burning steadily. Where are those damn fire trucks? He couldn't wait any longer. Perhaps someone had called already? But something had to be done now!

The weary man dashed across the street to the badly burning house, shielding his eyes from the sun. Whatever help his old bones could offer, at least he could give it a try.

The smell of burning oak wood irritated his nostrils. As he got to the other side of the street, he glanced up… seeing billows of black smoke spewing forth from the roof. The smoke concealed the red-hot fire that burned within.

He reached the front door of the house. Flames greeted his approach.

"Hello? Is anyone in there?" No response. Perhaps the people inside couldn't hear him? Rodney pushed hard against the front door. Locked. He glanced around trying to find something to break down the door. He spotted a metal pole lying on the ground. Rodney lifted the pole without a great deal of struggle and swung it at the door many times, hoping to smash it!

The door finally splintered, the aroma of chipped wood circulating in the air. Exhausted, He dropped the metal pole. It rolled away. The door was barely damaged. His tired muscles protested. The exhausted man glanced around, searching for a tool to use as a battering ram. A rock! Of course, that would help!

But where would he find a rock on this smooth tar-covered driveway? The exhausted Rodney searched the front yard of the house diligently for a perfect rock. A rock was finally discovered on the front lawn several feet away from the entrance. He lifted it, hoping it wasn't too heavy. Not bad. Size of a baseball. Rodney knew this would be just right. Not too heavy or light. The older man heaved himself against the door, rock in hand, his opposite shoulder pressing against the splintered door. He pushed several times until finally it gave way. During his pounding, the rock dented the doorknob. Rodney smiled to himself in satisfaction. Splinters of wood stuck into his clothes. He called out once more.

"Anyone in here?" he shouted, trying not to breathe in the smoke. Still no response. To think, the aging man had only moments ago felt so sad about a burnt pizza. Now he might be saving a life.

Rodney still wasn't sure if anyone was in there. Yet, the urge to do something rattled inside his head. Still no fire trucks! He pushed through the smoke while the scent of burning wood seeped deeper into his nostrils. Maybe the person's unconscious and can't hear me, the elder thought. But there was no time to consider that. He had to act now, *with or without the fire department.*

Finally, he worked his way to the kitchen. The main part of the fire seemed to have started in there. How ironic, he thought. He stared down at the floor and saw through the clouds of smoke a wrinkly old man lying on the floor, unconscious. The elder was small and lanky and was splayed on the kitchen floor as if he had just recently collapsed from breathing in the fumes. The man had white hair and was wearing plaid pajamas... and this fellow was *truly older*. Rodney felt the man was at least twenty years his senior.

The sixty-year-old bent down to lift the unconscious elder and immediately heard the sirens from earlier. *Finally,* he thought ... someone coming to help.

Though the unconscious body was light. It quickly became a struggle to carry him; he was now feeling the full effects from the fumes. Rodney stroked his mustache nervously, while he hefted the white-haired man over his shoulder, thinking this would help in carrying him from the burning building. He tripped over something on the floor, masked by increasingly billowing smoke. *We'll make it!,* he reassured himself. The mustached man coughed, breathing in the fumes. He was lying on the floor just out of reach of the door. With exhaustion setting in, Rodney knew they had to get out. He crawled tirelessly, the unconscious elder still on his back. Progress was slow, but gradually he advanced across the floor. The rapidly tiring elder, muscles straining, and pawing at the floor crawled on. What was left to travel? Ten feet? It may as well been a thousand.

With one final surge and heaving out an agonizing breath, Rodney plodded his way to the opened doorway, dragging himself and his unconscious burden onto the lawn outside.

Rodney rose slowly to his feet, wheezing from the fumes, then gazed down at the man he dragged to safety.

Firefighters had finally arrived. He eyed them with relief, he had likely saved a life. Exhausted, he collapsed, lying next to the man he had saved. Firefighters rushed to aid both of them. Rodney's two small dogs had somehow found a way across the street. They both licked his head as if congratulating him.

The victim, under the aid of the firefighters, finally regained consciousness. One of the firefighters whispered into the older man's ear, pointing to his rescuer.

"Thank you," the man wheezed, smiling up at Rodney.

Emergency workers carted the elderly man toward the ambulance, all of them nodding in approval at Rodney before departing. He then glanced happily at his two furry friends.

"Hey boys, how 'bout we make another pizza and bring some to our new friend when he comes home?" One of the dogs put its paws on his leg, as if in agreement.

"And yes, you both can have some too!"

Rodney rose and guided his two poodles across the street to begin making the pizza he would *not* burn this time.

Maybe he wasn't so old after all.

THE END

# HOUSE OF TREASURE

(A Vietnam veteran struggles for purpose in his new life.)

Phillip, a gruff looking forty-five-year-old Vietnam veteran, had just become a civilian.

The year was 1973. He thought of himself as someone who could survive almost anything. He liked being called a *survivalist*. But he wasn't without weakness. The war veteran suffered from shell shock and had horrible nightmares from brutal past battles. He had no friends and wished to feel truly home and not stuck in his life of sleepless nights.

Phillip was an adrenalin junky. Even after leaving military service, he craved challenges, for it gave him something to keep his mind sharp. He had heard of Hans Junson from a mercenary magazine, called Warriors of Fortune. Hans was also a French Foreign Legion veteran who was of Austrian origin. Phillip had seen the advertisement, looking for people tough enough to endure *being hunted* -- the reward of prevailing by finding a house in the forest during the night: the "Treasure House."

Not fully understanding the source of this vague treasure, Phillip accepted the advertised offer from Hans, meeting him in the clearing of a New England Forest. He had never met the Austrian till now, and beheld a man that towered over him, built like a human tank. Now, this Vietnam vet was no scrawny weakling, but he certainly felt like one in comparison to the powerfully built legionnaire.

"So you've come here hoping for some treasure?" Hans spouted gruffly.

Phillip nodded strongly.

"Well then, this won't be easy," grumbled the Austrian. "No one has yet to claim the treasure. You have an hour head start!" the giant proclaimed. Hans sniffed the air around the American. Phillip noticed this and thought it strange.

Not knowing what to fully expect in the forest, Phillip was aware that he needed tools for survival; yet, he had failed to bring his gun. He truly hadn't believed he would have needed it. He didn't think this would be a *lethal* hunt. He did bring his favorite knife, however; that he had once used in combat only as a last resort. The knife had a six inch blade and he called the weapon "Lucky," because it had saved him in the past.

The Austrian gestured for him to go. Phillip dashed cautiously out into the unknown.

Hans glanced at his watch, expecting the hour to move faster.

****

Deep in the forest, Phillip scrambled to find additional items he might use. It was almost pitch black, albeit a full moon just breaking through the canopy of trees. Phillip's foot grazed something hard; he nearly tripped over it. The former soldier glanced down, trying to discover what it might be. *A rifle.* The dim light of the moon had revealed it. It was an old-time Henry rifle. He picked it up and checked the chamber. Empty. The stout man dropped the rifle on the spot. Why was this deadly weapon left behind? Phillip pondered what had happened to the people before him. Had they been killed? He realized when he'd met the Austrian, the man was no one to trifle with.

Phillip didn't know if he was anywhere close to the house he was supposed to find. The faint light from the moon provided a view of the moss on the trees. Phillip now knew where north was, based on the thickness of the moss' location, but did he really know north was the right way?

This legionnaire must have been good at hunting, thought the American.

Hans Junson clearly had demonstrated that darkness did not slow his pace; the man rushed forward, tracking his prey like a wild beast. Hans was scanning the ground and he occasionally sniffed like a wolf, catching his quarry's scent. The Foreign

Legionnaire pulled out a knife similar to the fleeing man's and regarded the deadly dagger, sensing his prey was close by.

****

Phillip stepped slowly through the forest as he tried to avoid making a sound. He wished he had brought moccasins; they would not have made so much noise. Every step the war vet took gave an audible crunch as leaves crumbled underfoot. This was not what he'd expected to deal with when he'd started. His eyes squeezed together with each step.

*He didn't notice a leghold trap, that appeared preset.*

The jaws closed on his foot! Phillip used all his strength and willpower not to scream. He searched the moonlit ground for a stick to shove between his teeth. The pain was excruciating.

Great! thought Phillip. He used his knife to pry the leghold trap open, but the spring resisted the knife. Were these springs going to break the knife or break his ankle? Phillip did not want to know. Finally, after using every pull of his strength, he pried the leghold trap open, enough to jerk his leg free. Blood spilled down his ankle and he knew it would leave a trail for Hans to follow. Why had he neglected to bring his first aid kit along with him? Dumb!

****

The Austrian's ears pricked toward the sky as if trying to detect sounds of agony; he had no idea that Phillip had been caught in the trap. The legionnaire grew worried that his quarry had evaded it.

"You won't make it to the house alive!" Hans yelled menacingly, hoping to quell any delusions of escape the fleeing man might entertain.

Phillip wanted to retort, but knew it would give away his position, which seemed close to Hans' booming voice. Need to move carefully and catch him from behind, he thought. He shook his head after pondering that. The Austrian stepped forward with an audible thump!

Phillip thought back to when he was in the Vietnam jungle, hiding from the Viet Cong, and how the feeling of being hunted unsettled him. If there were traps out in this forest, Hans likely knew where they all were. Phillip thought that maybe he could plant a trap himself for the Austrian. But with what? He had only his hunting knife. A *vine trap*, maybe that could snare the big man. Images of the legionnaire hanging upside down helplessly from a tree branch gave Phillip a chuckle.

The ex-legionnaire was on the prowl and sniffed the ground for his prey's telltale scent. Hans smirked. He knew where Phillip was, but purposely looked away in the opposite direction. The foreign legionnaire stood above the crouching form of the American hiding fearfully in the bush.

Phillip glanced up toward the ex-legionnaire. Why was he just standing there? Was the hunter playing with his victim? Waiting to be attacked cut deeper into his nerves.

Hans trotted away. Before getting too far, he glanced back in the vet's direction, but not directly at him.

The hunted man took his knife and started carving a spear from a fallen branch. Bleeding all the more, he continued without making a sound. The stout man thought the Austrian might have detected him by now. Had the hunter moved to strike from behind? The American scanned the dark, ready to strike.

No time to think. Time only to act.

"Hans, you dirty dog, you'll never beat me to that Treasure House!" Phillip bellowed.

Hans spun round and jogged over to where he'd heard the voice.

Phillip knew he was coming. He threw the spear. Missed! No choice now; he had to use his knife. The

Austrian was rapidly closing the gap. Phillip ducked into the brush, knife at the ready. Hans, in a reckless rush, had not noticed his concealed prey. The American leapt out from the brush the light of moon now dimmed. Phillip stabbed the huge man in the shoulder.

The American ignored Hans' moans of pain and limped away with a brief smirk of victory.

****

The fleeing man had reached a clearing in the trees. A reddish glow from the rising sun peeked above the horizon. Out in the middle of the clearing was the *Treasure House*: a beautiful cottage with a halo of reddish light emanating from it. Being hunted had exhausted the Vietnam vet. He wanted that treasure more than anything now. His skills had been utterly tested. Was he really going to get there? But he collapsed to his knees in exhaustion.

Phillip struggled to get back up, groaning. *He had to make it to that house.* The vet limped onward, wincing at his still bleeding ankle. He had a good hundred yards to go. Perhaps he might find something to heal his wounds there.

But why hadn't the legionnaire just killed him when he'd had the chance? And where was that brute now?

****

Hans tugged at the knife still embedded in his shoulder. He knew it would hurt terribly and it would create a lot of blood, but he wanted to get it out. He reached into his pack and grabbed gauze from his first aid kit, which he had remember to bring; he quickly applied it around the knife. Blood seeped through and turned the bandage red. This American really enjoyed the struggle. It was not at all what he thought he'd be dealing with when he'd first met him. Hans marched forward with a purpose.

The tough American limped on. He glanced back, Hans was no longer there. *The sly hunter had disappeared.* Why did the brute not stab me when I ran by?

"You should give up now; you have no chance!" Hans yelled between painful grunts.

Phillip glanced up to see Hans stepping out from behind the house. I'm never going to make it, he thought. He's going to kill me now. That treasure must be very important to him.

"Phillip, stop!" Hans yelled.

The American ignored the Austrian's yells. He did find it strange that the hunter used his name for the first time. Phillip collapsed again when he reached the door of the "Treasure House." He had made it! The hunted man pulled on the door. Locked. Dammit, the veteran thought.

Hans strode forward, his knife held high as he approached the vet. The hunted man put up his fists, ready to fight.

"Put your hands down Phillip, I'm not going to kill you," the Austrian proclaimed. "You have passed the test." Hans dropped his arm not putting his knife away. "I'm here to give you the treasure!" the legionnaire boomed proudly.

How could this be? Hans had the treasure the whole time? Phillip didn't understand. He raised his hands again, not completely trusting Hans to not spare him now.

"*I'm* the treasure… *my friendship*," the hunter said. "Welcome to my home." No one but you has ever earned that treasure. You've bested me; we can now be friends," the Austrian said.

This was what Phillip had wanted too; *a friend*. Someone who actually understood him. "What ever happened to all the others?"

The legionnaire gestured to the house. "Come, let's patch up." "The others went home with nothing. *They all failed*," Hans said with a smile. Phillip relaxed and put down his fists.

The Vietnam vet followed Hans into the house, every bit as delighted to have earned a true friend.

## THE END

## WHERE IS HOME?

(First published in Conceit Magazine, April 2022)

(A woman wakes in the dead of night, convinced an intruder is in her home.)

Stephanie woke with a start! Some potent six sense that had always alerted her in the past when danger lurked ----- or the harsh *thump* that had echoed throughout the house --- was what had jolted her awake. Her midnight black hair ruffled in the slight breeze coming from an open window. Regardless, she knew something was amiss in her home as an air of abrupt menace seized hold of her. Stephanie's face filled with terror. Sweat poured down her thirty-year-old face. She reached for her glasses. They immediately fogged up from the moisture of her breath in the now chilly room. She wished she'd closed that damn window. Her mind flashed back instantly, instinctively, to when she had returned home, laden with bundles from shopping ... *and she had forgotten to lock the front door afterwards.* She had even told herself to bolt it after putting down the groceries on the counter, but had been distracted when the wind from the open window had whipped her long hair into her face and she had forgotten entirely. Now, of course, she recalled every detail of what she had done instead of locking the door immediately, as was her usual habit -- knowing inner city living as she did.

Another thump!

Stephanie's hopes of it all having been just her imagination were washed away in an instant. *An intruder was in her house.* Who had sneaked in? she wondered, her face still moist from the fearful sweat. She pushed back the covers and crept slowly, quietly, out of the bed, stepping cautiously in the dark toward the door that led from her bedroom. Whoever had invaded her home had to still be in the living room, based on the distance of the noises she'd heard.

She groped about in the dark before finding and putting one hand on the doorknob, the other on a dinner fork on a nearby table. She had forgotten to wash the fork from her breakfast in bed earlier that morning. The fork was smeared in the leftovers of egg she had eaten. Though it was just a fork, it still had *four sharp tines*. She could put it to good use.

Stephanie, fork in hand, smirked and listened at the bedroom door. Was the villain about to steal something… perhaps even kill her? She shivered at the thought. The black-haired woman didn't want to know. The squeaking of footsteps on the other side alerted her that whoever it was had entered the kitchen. The creaking door emitted a sound of the release of pressure. *The intruder had found the refrigerator.* An influx of fury filled her and she threw open the bedroom door, yelling like a warrior ready for battle! *No one was going to steal her hard-made food.*

Stephanie's free hand reached for the hallway light switch and flipped it on. Then, with both hands, she raised the fork, ready to thrust it into whoever had broken in. Stephanie caught sight of a figure, seemingly scared and stumbling away into the living room. The short figure had left the refrigerator door open, leaving a dim light illuminating the floor. But where had this mysterious intruder gone?

As if asking the room to reveal the culprit, a loud crash indicated where the sneak had gone. The prowler seemed to have tripped over an ottoman Stephanie frequently left in the middle of the floor. Apparently the foot rest had upended the intruder. Was that crash the same that had woken her? Had this intruder slipped in through the living room window? Why not the unlocked door? No time for thinking now… Stephanie had to confront whoever it was. She scampered in pursuit into the living room. The light was dim from the window there.

But the moon was shining through the glass. Her eyes adjusted and could finally depict the figure. *It was just a boy; he had to be at least ten*! His clothes were tattered; signs of spilled stew that were once contained in a plastic box now covered the living room floor.

"Who are you?" Stephanie demanded. The child-figure groaned as it stood up. And from out of the shadows, a small boy stepped into the dim light "You didn't answer me," she said with a growing frustration.

"I'm Juan, please don't hurt me!" the child exclaimed, recoiling as if expecting to be hit or stabbed by the dangerous dinner fork she wielded. In the faint light, Stephanie noticed the state of the child's clothes and how skinny he looked.

Juan stepped forward sheepishly and handed over to her the now empty container. "I'm sorry about the stew, but I'm so hungry," Juan said weakly. The aroma of the spilled stew now permeated the entire room. Stephanie frowned at the odor. *She had really wanted that stew*. Now it was all but being absorbed by the carpet. Should she discipline this ragged boy... or somehow help him? This wasn't a real burglar, it was a hungry child desperate for food. The upset woman, while pondering her next move, didn't notice Juan bolting to the window. She glanced up just in time as the boy had his foot on the back of the couch by the window.

"Where do you think you're going? We're not done here!" Stephanie grumbled. The ten-year-old child turned back, hiding his face. She pointed at the ground as if prompting the young Hispanic boy to come over to the spot she'd indicated. He shuffled toward it.

"Why are you stealing?" she proclaimed, glaring at the young boy.

"I just need food. I'm so sorry!" Juan exclaimed sadly.

Stephanie concluded that Juan was very likely poverty stricken ... maybe even living off the street. She thought back to her own childhood where she herself had sometimes struggled to find food.

"Listen, you shouldn't steal, but how about I make you something to eat instead?" Stephanie said pleasantly.

Do I trust her? his face seemed to say.

"You can sleep on my couch. Tomorrow we'll try to get you some help. The dark-haired woman was familiar with the local social services. Stephanie had once worked for social services, wanting to give back for helping her when she herself had struggled. "They're people around in town who can help you more than I could all by myself," Stephanie explained. "But, what about your parents?"

He looked down at his torn-up shoes, not glancing up at her. "My parents abandoned me, I'm all alone. They didn't want me," the young boy said trying to hide his tears.

The young woman had never had children, but she definitely felt this boy's pain.

Stephanie closed the window and locked the door that she should have locked from the beginning. She tried hugging the boy, but he flinched. He clearly wasn't ready for that.

But he was exhausted and eyed the nearby couch. Stephanie gestured warmly toward the couch, smiling as she did. Juan nodded tentatively, then made his way over to it, where he laid down. Convinced now that he was safe and this woman could be trusted.

The young boy gave a tiny smile. Stephanie sat next to him. Tomorrow, she planned to make sure this child got all the care he needed.

THE END

Made in the USA
Middletown, DE
27 July 2024

58036273R00029